P9-CFT-098

*To all the kings and queens—former,
present, and future—of Night to Shine and our
courageous W15H children and families.
We love you!*

**BRONCO AND FRIENDS**

All Scripture quotations are taken from the Holy Bible, New Living Translation, copyright © 1996, 2004, 2015 by Tyndale House Foundation. Used by permission of Tyndale House Publishers, a division of Tyndale House Ministries, Carol Stream, Illinois 60188. All rights reserved.

Text and illustrations copyright © 2021 by Timothy R. Tebow

All rights reserved.

Published in the United States by WaterBrook, an imprint of Random House, a division of Penguin Random House LLC.

**WATERBROOK®** and its deer colophon are registered trademarks of Penguin Random House LLC.

ISBN 978-0-593-23204-0
Ebook ISBN 978-0-593-23205-7

The Library of Congress catalog record is available at https://lccn.loc.gov/2020027897.

Printed in the United States of America

waterbrookmultnomah.com

10 9 8 7 6 5 4 3 2

First Edition

Book and jacket design: Mia Johnson
Cover and interior illustrations: Jane Chapman

**SPECIAL SALES** Most WaterBrook books are available at special quantity discounts when purchased in bulk by corporations, organizations, and special-interest groups. Custom imprinting or excerpting can also be done to fit special needs. For information, please email specialmarketscms@penguinrandomhouse.com.

BRONCO *AND* FRIENDS

# A Party to Remember

# Tim Tebow

with A. J. Gregory

## Illustrated by Jane Chapman

WATERBROOK

"Wake up!" Squirrel shrieked. "The party is tonight. Do you have your puzzle piece?"

Bronco squinted one eye open.

"I've got mine!"

Bronco patted the soft grass. Where are my glasses?

Suddenly he remembered something important.
Days earlier, he'd received a card. It read:

Come find our special party
full of music, fun, and treats.
We'll have a big ol' puzzle,
though it won't yet be complete.
Yours is the missing piece.
That is no mystery.
You'll find it when you realize
you are made purposefully.

Because Bronco had terrible vision, he didn't think he was special enough to go to the party. So he'd thrown out the invitation.

"I guess I'm not going," Bronco told Squirrel. Yet deep inside his heart, he really, really wanted to.

"At least try to find your puzzle piece! It's out there somewhere. We all have one. You don't want to miss this party, Bronco!"

Bronco's heart began to race.

He slapped on his glasses and pawed through his dog dish. No puzzle piece. He dug around the yard. Nothing.

Using his special gift of sniff, with his ears attuned to the tiniest sound, Bronco widened his search.

"Doe-ray-me-far-sew-la-tea!"

Chipmunk called out to Bronco,
"I'm practicing my scales for
the karaoke contest at the party!
I want to win."

"Wow! Great pitch!"

As he walked on, Bronco saw Pig testing out his tap shoes.

"Oh no!" Robin called. "Watch out, Bronco!"

Bronco tumbled onto something soft.

Chelsie the rabbit sighed deeply. "I'm so sorry. My long ears are always in the way."

Bronco gathered Chelsie's ears off the path and gently placed them behind her.

"Are you going to the party?" he asked.

"I'd like to," Chelsie answered, "but I don't know where it is. And, anyway, I have no one to go with."

"Why not come with me?
It's always better together."

Bronco's ears twitched.
"Is someone crying?"

Ethan wiped away a tear.

"What's wrong?" Bronco asked.

"I'm supposed to go to the party, but my
wing is broken. I can't carry my puzzle
piece. And I definitely can't fly!"

"Hop on one of my ears and come with us," Chelsie offered.
"Bronco is showing me the way."

Ethan hopped up and giggled, tickled by Chelsie's long and fuzzy ears.

The trio traveled on together. Bronco sniffed ahead for his missing puzzle piece.

"ACHOoo!"

Bronco said, "What was that?"

Embarrassed, a goat slunk to the ground.

"Are you okay, Alexis?" chirped Ethan.

"I sneeze too loud and scare everyone away," the goat said.

"I've been invited to the party, but I don't think anyone would want me there!"

"We do!" Bronco said.

On the gang walked. Bronco's nose led the way, searching for the party and his puzzle piece.

"My ears are so heavy," Chelsie fussed. "I don't know how much longer I can hop!"

"But I really want to go to the party!" Ethan whispered.

"I'm so hungry—achoOO!" Alexis interrupted herself with another sneeze.

"Let's go, friends! We can't stop now!"

But as Bronco sniffed onward, he looked at his friends and sighed. *What if I let them down?*

"This is too hard," Bronco yelped. "I don't think I'll ever find my puzzle piece, and I don't know the way to the party!"

"You can do this, Bronco!" his friends chorused.

"I wouldn't even be here if it weren't for you," Chelsie said.

"I wouldn't be here if it weren't for you finding Chelsie," Ethan chirped.

"I wouldn't be here if you hadn't invited me along," Alexis bleated.

*Maybe I am here for a reason!*
Bronco thought.

"ACHOOOO!"

Alexis sneezed so big and so loud,
the branches swished open and . . .

Wait, what is that?

"I smell pizza!"

"Are those lights?"

"I hear music!"

"The party!"

Critters of all kinds paraded down a velvety red carpet with glittery lights. It was a celebration like no other. They couldn't wait to go inside!

Bronco's heart fell. He still hadn't found his puzzle piece.

Sadly, Bronco turned to leave.

Colby, the handsome host in his natural tux, waved at Bronco. "Looking for this?"

The pooch leapt with joy.

"That's mine!"

"Bronco, you helped each of your friends get here today, thanks to your special gifts of sniff and hearing.

Each creature is born unique.
Our differences make us special.
And someone special, like you, is
always able to do great things."

Bronco paused beside a grand table
with the giant puzzle.

His was the missing piece everyone
was waiting for!

"Are you ready to celebrate?"
Colby asked.

Now it was time to party!

"Hop on!" Chelsie announced to Ethan and his tiny friends as she flapped her giant ears.

Alexis gobbled up some tasty treats before she needed to sneeze again.

"Bronco," Colby said,
"I heard you have a side
hustle mixing beats!"

"Just show me where
the DJ booth is!"

Later that night, under a beautiful starry sky,
the four friends walked home. They beamed and
giggled as they shared their favorite moments
from their party to remember.

"We are God's masterpiece.
He has created us anew in
Christ Jesus, so we can do the good
things he planned for us long ago."

Ephesians 2:10

You are unique.
You are special.
And you are wonderful.